HEROES OF THE SURF

A rescue story based on true events

ELISA CARBONE ✳ NANCY CARPENTER

VIKING

An Imprint of Penguin Group (USA) Inc.

VIKING
Published by Penguin Group
Penguin Young Readers Group, 345 Hudson Street, New York, New York 10014, U.S.A.
Penguin Group (Canada), 90 Eglinton Avenue East, Suite 700, Toronto, Ontario, Canada M4P 2Y3 (a division of Pearson Penguin Canada Inc.)
Penguin Books Ltd, 80 Strand, London WC2R 0RL, England
Penguin Ireland, 25 St Stephen's Green, Dublin 2, Ireland (a division of Penguin Books Ltd)
Penguin Group (Australia), 250 Camberwell Road, Camberwell, Victoria 3124, Australia (a division of Pearson Australia Group Pty Ltd)
Penguin Books India Pvt Ltd, 11 Community Centre, Panchsheel Park, New Delhi – 110 017, India
Penguin Group (NZ), 67 Apollo Drive, Rosedale, Auckland 0632, New Zealand (a division of Pearson New Zealand Ltd.)
Penguin Books (South Africa) (Pty) Ltd, 24 Sturdee Avenue, Rosebank, Johannesburg 2196, South Africa

Penguin Books Ltd, Registered Offices: 80 Strand, London WC2R 0RL, England

First published in 2012 by Viking, a division of Penguin Young Readers Group

1 3 5 7 9 10 8 6 4 2

Text copyright © Elisa Carbone, 2012
Illustrations copyright © Nancy Carpenter, 2012
All rights reserved

LIBRARY OF CONGRESS CATALOGING-IN-PUBLICATION DATA
Carbone, Elisa Lynn.
Heroes of the surf / by Elisa Carbone.
p. cm.
Summary: When the huge steamship on which they are traveling runs aground off the New Jersey coast in 1882, two boys and their families are
among the passengers dramatically rescued by members of the U.S. Life Saving Service. Includes notes about the event on which the story is based.
ISBN 978-0-670-06312-3 (hardcover)
[1. Shipwrecks—Fiction. 2. United States. Life-Saving Service—Fiction. 3. New Jersey—History—19th century—Fiction.] I. Title.
PZ7.C1865He 2012
[E]—dc23
2011012218

Manufactured in China
Set in Clarendon

ALWAYS LEARNING   PEARSON

To the Heroes of the Surf:
the surfmen of the Deal Beach, Long Branch, and Shark River Life Saving stations.
And to my granddaughter, Emma Lynn Nugent
—E. C.

For Kieran
—N. C.

May 13, 1882

Our steamship, *Pliny*, left Brazil three weeks ago on April 22—I know because I wrote it in my pirate logbook.

    The *Pliny* is the biggest ship I've ever been on. Captain Mitchell says she's nearly 300 feet long and weighs over 1,000 tons. She's got decks as wide as a house and steam engines that groan all day and night, pushing us through the open seas. I've counted thirty-six crew and twenty-five passengers on board.

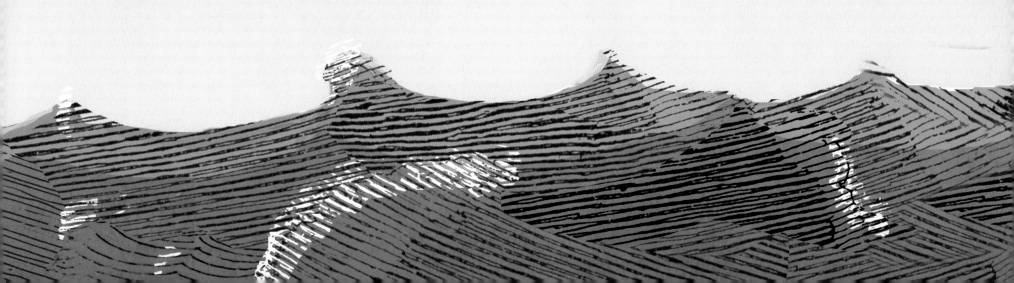

That includes me and Sis, Mama and Papa, my friend Pedro and his papa, and seven other children. The noisiest passenger is also the smallest: Mr. and Mrs. Smith's baby daughter, Sarah. She is almost always crying. I don't blame her—I'll bet she is seasick like most people are.

Mama, Papa, and Sis think we're on an ordinary steamer bound for New York City. My friend Pedro and I know better.

"Ship ahoy," I call out. "We'll plunder their stores!"

"We'll take their gold," cries Pedro.

"Then we'll sink them to the bottom of the ocean!" I shout.

Black storm clouds are rolling in.

"All pirates below," Captain Mitchell orders.
"Rough seas ahead."

"Aye aye, sir," we say.

Fat raindrops begin to plop onto the deck.

I ask Mama if I can sleep in Pedro's bunk
tonight.

"Don't forget your nightshirt," she says.

It will be fun to spend the night with Pedro
and his papa.

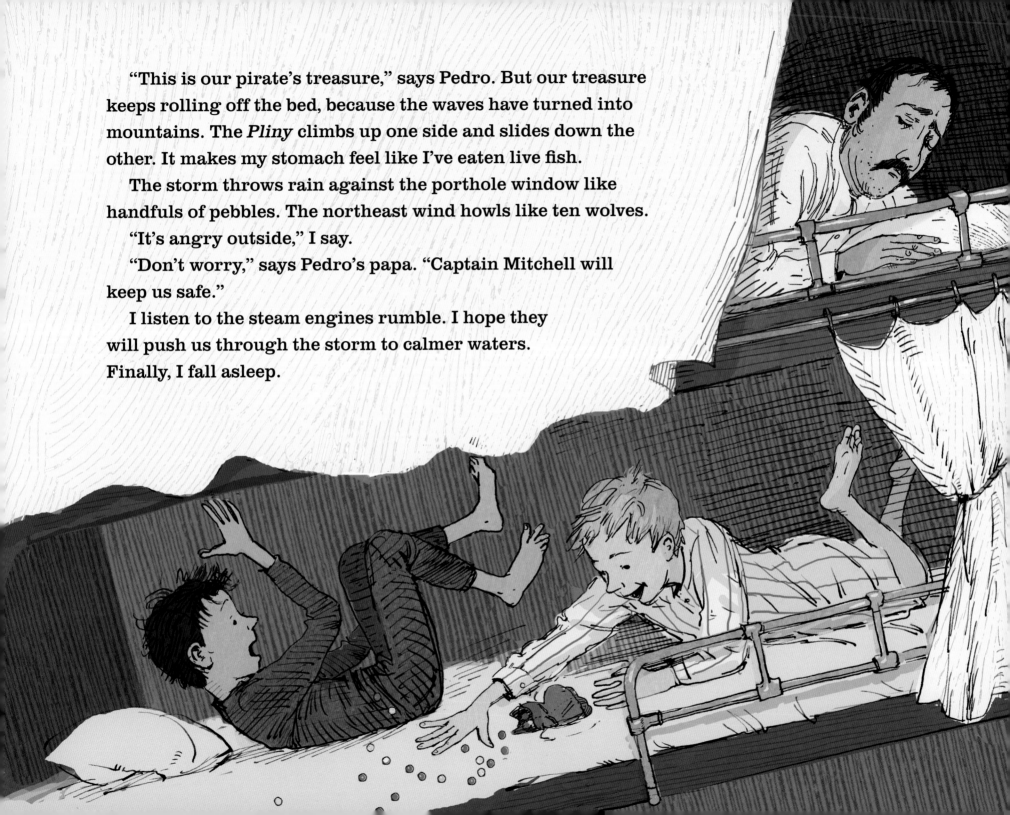

"This is our pirate's treasure," says Pedro. But our treasure keeps rolling off the bed, because the waves have turned into mountains. The *Pliny* climbs up one side and slides down the other. It makes my stomach feel like I've eaten live fish.

The storm throws rain against the porthole window like handfuls of pebbles. The northeast wind howls like ten wolves.

"It's angry outside," I say.

"Don't worry," says Pedro's papa. "Captain Mitchell will keep us safe."

I listen to the steam engines rumble. I hope they will push us through the storm to calmer waters. Finally, I fall asleep.

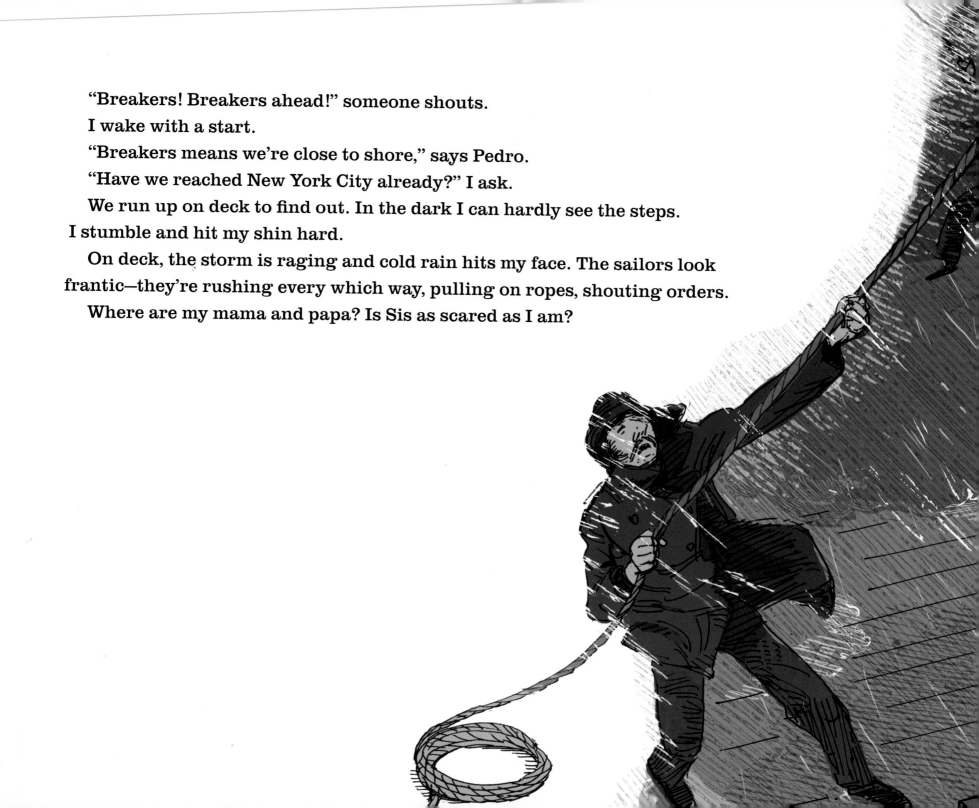

"Breakers! Breakers ahead!" someone shouts.

I wake with a start.

"Breakers means we're close to shore," says Pedro.

"Have we reached New York City already?" I ask.

We run up on deck to find out. In the dark I can hardly see the steps. I stumble and hit my shin hard.

On deck, the storm is raging and cold rain hits my face. The sailors look frantic—they're rushing every which way, pulling on ropes, shouting orders.

Where are my mama and papa? Is Sis as scared as I am?

Suddenly, *WHAM!* the *Pliny* jolts as if Black Beard himself has just punched her in the belly. Pedro and I slide and smack—*bang*—into the bulwark.

"We're grounded," cries the first mate. "We've hit a shoal!"

Now the *Pliny* can't roll with the waves. She's stuck like a rock in tar, and she's tipped like she's ready to fall. Seawater crashes over her deck. I start to slide with the water. I'm going overboard!

"Hold on!" Pedro yells.
I grab his hand just in time.

We scramble onto the forecastle deck. The gray sky is turning lighter. I can see Mama, Papa, Sis, and Pedro's papa. They're climbing onto the bridge. They look scared, too. Sis is wailing. My hands are so cold I can barely hold on.

There is so much shouting, so much confusion. I wonder if anyone knows what we should do.

"Lower the lifeboats!" someone shouts.

"Good," says Pedro. "Now we will be saved."

We struggle toward the lifeboats on the port side of the *Pliny*. Dark monster waves lash at their hulls. One wave thunders in, taller than a house, and I hear a woman scream. The wave rips the lifeboats loose and splinters them like matchboxes.

"What will we do now?!" I cry.

From the forecastle deck a rocket shoots into the air, red with fire.

"The captain is signaling for help," says Pedro. His teeth are chattering with cold and fear.

Then, over the pounding of the waves, over the howling of the wind, over the shouts of the sailors and the wailing of the children, I hear it: the silence.

"The engines," cries the first mate. "The sea has burst the hatches and killed the engines!"

Now we're sure to sink. I want to be with Mama and Papa and Sis when we go down.

But before I even take a step, Pedro grabs me and yanks me back to the rail. "Look," he says, pointing.

At first I think it's a strange wave. Then I see it in the gray morning light: *Land*. There's a sandy beach, a steep bluff, something moving on the bluff.

"They're . . . men," I say. They look spooky in the half light. I count them. ". . . five, six, seven."

Then I see something else. They have a cannon.

"Are they . . . ?" I ask.

"Could they be . . . ?" Pedro begins.

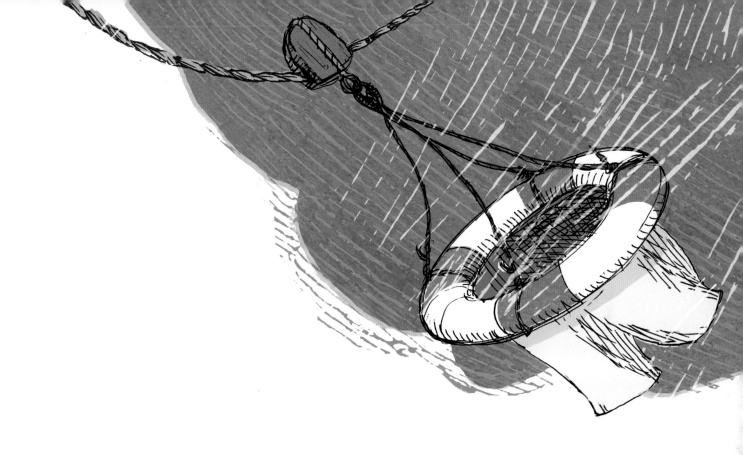

A leaden weight and rope come whizzing over our heads. The rope catches in the rigging, then flutters down like a bird on the deck.

"It's the rescue line," the first mate calls out.

Pedro and I stare at each other. The rescue line? Those men are not pirates at all.

"Haul in the whip-line," the first mate orders.

"Fasten the hawser to the foremast."

"Here comes the breeches buoy!"

It comes swinging toward us hanging from the rope: a life preserver with a pair of short pants attached.

"Women and children first," Captain Mitchell shouts over the wind.

He helps Mrs. Smith climb into the breeches buoy. She is holding baby Sarah.

The breeches buoy swings, and Mrs. Smith cries out, "Oh no! I'll drop her in the ocean!"

Her husband takes the baby from her. "I will bring her to you," he promises.

Now the men on shore pull the ropes and Mrs. Smith swings over the crashing waves. They haul in rhythm together to make the breeches buoy glide through the air toward shore.

"Who are those men?" I ask Captain Mitchell.

"Heroes of the surf," he answers. "The surfmen of the United States Life-Saving Service."

Mr. Smith rides the breeches buoy next, with baby Sarah tucked under his coat. She wails all the way to shore, her cries mixing with the shrieking of the wind. But Mr. Smith does not drop her, and soon they are safe on land.

"Anthony, you're next," Captain Mitchell orders.

I gulp. "Me?!"

I climb into the breeches buoy. My knees are shaking. I hold on so tightly my fingers feel like crab claws.

"I will follow you, *amigo*," says Pedro.

I swing out into open space. Below me, waves crash and twist like angry snakes. Will the ropes hold? Will I be dropped into the sea? The wind slaps my cold, wet nightshirt against my skin. I look up at the men on shore. "Soon I will be there," I tell myself.

"Help him down."

"He's shivering; get a blanket."

The surfmen lift me down with their strong arms.

"Welcome to Deal Beach, New Jersey," says one of the surfmen. He looks tired, but he's smiling at me.

"Thank you, sir," I say.

He wraps a wool blanket around my shoulders. The wool feels scratchy on my neck, and the sand seems to move under me, as if the waves are still there. But I am on land—safe, solid land.

When I look around, I see that more people
have gathered, with still more arriving—men
in top hats and even ladies with their shawls
wrapped tightly. It looks as if the whole town has
turned out for the rescue.

The surfmen keep pulling the breeches buoy
ropes. They bring in Sis, then Mama, and then
Papa. I hug them each so hard my chest hurts. I
pretend those are raindrops on my cheeks, but
really they are tears of relief.

By the time Pedro's papa arrives, the sky is light and a wagon is waiting to take us to the Long Branch Life Saving Station. The station smells of hot coffee brewing and fresh biscuits baking—the station cook has been busy.

We pull dry clothes out of a big box. The sleeves of my new shirt flop like elephant trunks, and I make Pedro and Sis laugh.

Captain Mitchell sits down to eat with us. He lifts his mug of coffee. "I propose a toast," he says. "To the heroes of the surf. Everyone on board the *Pliny* has been rescued."

We all raise our mugs to celebrate.

We pass around a plate of steaming hot biscuits and another with thick slices of ham. I'm so hungry I stuff my mouth with huge bites, and when I grin, biscuit sticks out.

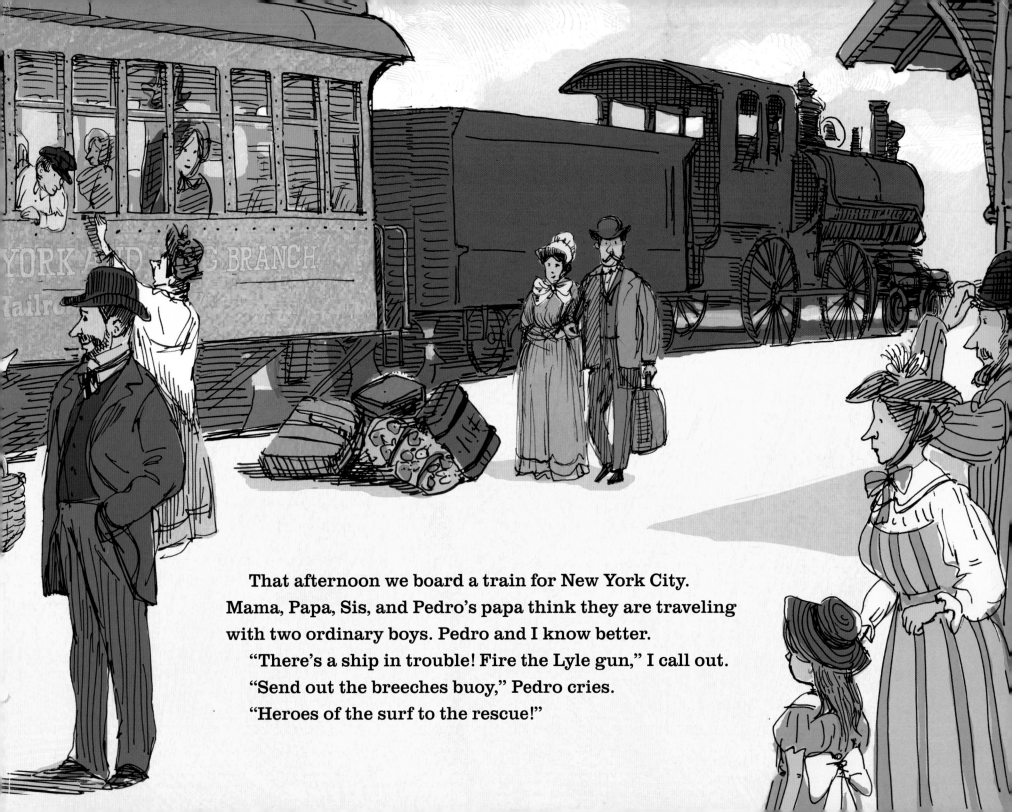

That afternoon we board a train for New York City.
Mama, Papa, Sis, and Pedro's papa think they are traveling
with two ordinary boys. Pedro and I know better.

"There's a ship in trouble! Fire the Lyle gun," I call out.

"Send out the breeches buoy," Pedro cries.

"Heroes of the surf to the rescue!"

AFTERWORD

On April 22, 1882, the British steamship *Pliny* left Rio de Janeiro, Brazil, headed for New York City. It carried a cargo of coffee and hides, along with the crew and passengers, ten or eleven of them children (reports vary). On the night of May 13, a storm caused the *Pliny* to run aground off the coast of New Jersey.

The Life-Saving Service stations were already closed for the summer, but because of the rough weather several surfmen wisely kept watch. At 3:10 a.m., they saw the *Pliny*'s distress signal. They immediately began to rally men and equipment, and by 4:50 a.m. the rescue was underway.

Though the rescue began with seven surfmen, word of a wreck with children aboard passed quickly through the nearby towns. Soon there were Life-Saving Service crewmen from the Deal Beach, Long Branch, and Shark River stations and a crowd of townspeople operating the breeches buoy and helping the cold, wet passengers find comfort.

Anthony, Pedro, and the other passengers and crew were able to change into dry clothes thanks to boxes of clothing collected by the Women's National Relief Association. Though there were no female surfmen, this was a way women played an important role in the Life-Saving Service.

The names of people on the *Pliny* come from the wreck report and passenger list. I have named Anthony and Pedro after their fathers, as children's names were not recorded.

Although in the story as I have written it, the passengers and crew were brought to one life saving service station, in actuality some were brought to other stations nearby, and most of the passengers went to the home of Mr. Samuel Hendrickson before taking a train to New York City.

In the early years of the Life-Saving Service, crewmen were issued equipment but no uniforms. As a result, when the Lyle gun—which looked and sounded just like a small cannon—was fired for the breeches buoy rescue, sailors and passengers sometimes thought they were being attacked by pirates! When the Life-Saving Service eventually issued official uniforms, this helped to clarify the situation.

In 1915, the USLSS was combined with the Revenue Cutter Service to become the United States Coast Guard. The Coast Guard is still in operation today, saving lives on dangerous waters.